For Dennis, Christine, Mark, Elsie and Jim . . .G.A.

Library of Congress Cataloging-in-Publication Data

Alexander, Claire.
Small Florence, piggy pop star / written and illustrated by Claire Alexander.
p. cm.
Summary: Florence, a young pig, is too shy to sing in front of her sisters but gathers
her courage at a singing competition when they lose their nerve.
ISBN 978-0-8075-7455-3
[1. Singers—Fiction. 2. Bashfulness—Fiction. 3. Self-confidence—Fiction. 4. Sisters—Fiction. 5. Pigs—Fiction.] I. Title.
PZ7.A37666Sm 2010
[E]—dc22

2009023624

10 9 8 7 6 5 4 3 2 1 HK 14 13 12 11 10 09

First published in Great Britain in 2009 by Gullane Children's Books.

The artwork for this book was rendered in pencil with acrylic paint on paper.

For more information about Albert Whitman & Company,
visit our web site at www.albertwhitman.com.

# Small Florence

*Piggy Pop Star!*

CLAIRE ALEXANDER

Albert Whitman & Company
Chicago, Illinois

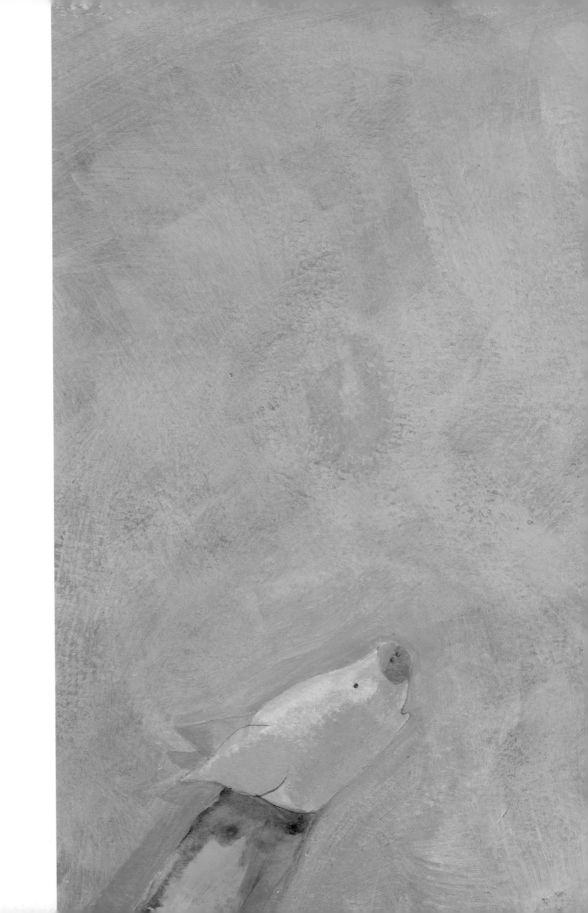

Florence was a small pig.
She was a happy soul,
if a little shy at times.

She had two older sisters.

"What's small, pink, and squeaky?"

"Florence!"

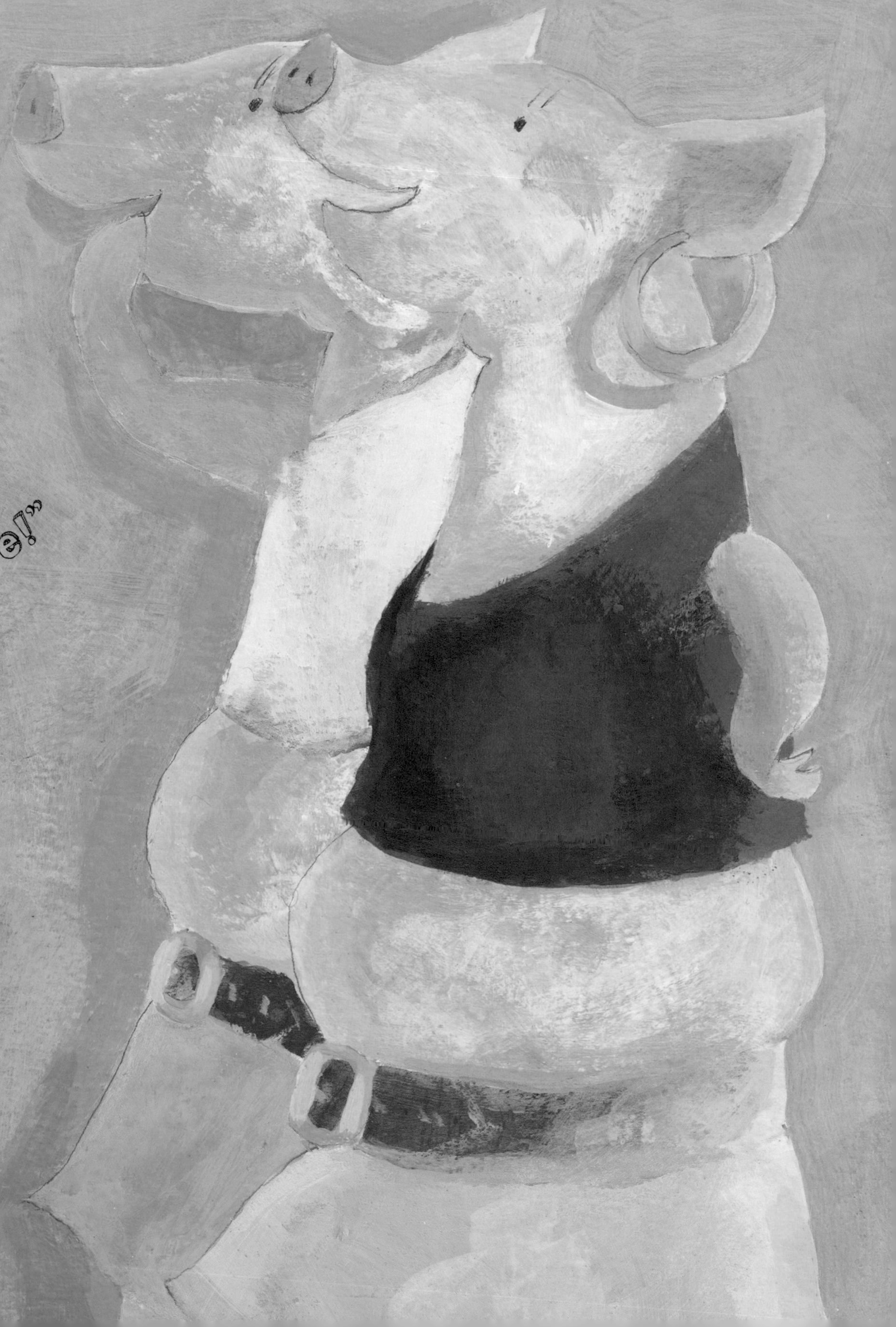

Florence thought her sisters were very
lucky. They were taking singing
lessons from Jazzy-Funk Mutt,
the cool singing teacher.

"Ham it up, sisters! Smooth!"

Florence dreamed of
one day becoming a piggy
pop star on television.

She sang to herself in secret. She sang
under the covers of her bed at night and
she sang in the bath every morning.

After a while, she plucked up the courage to sing to her friends...

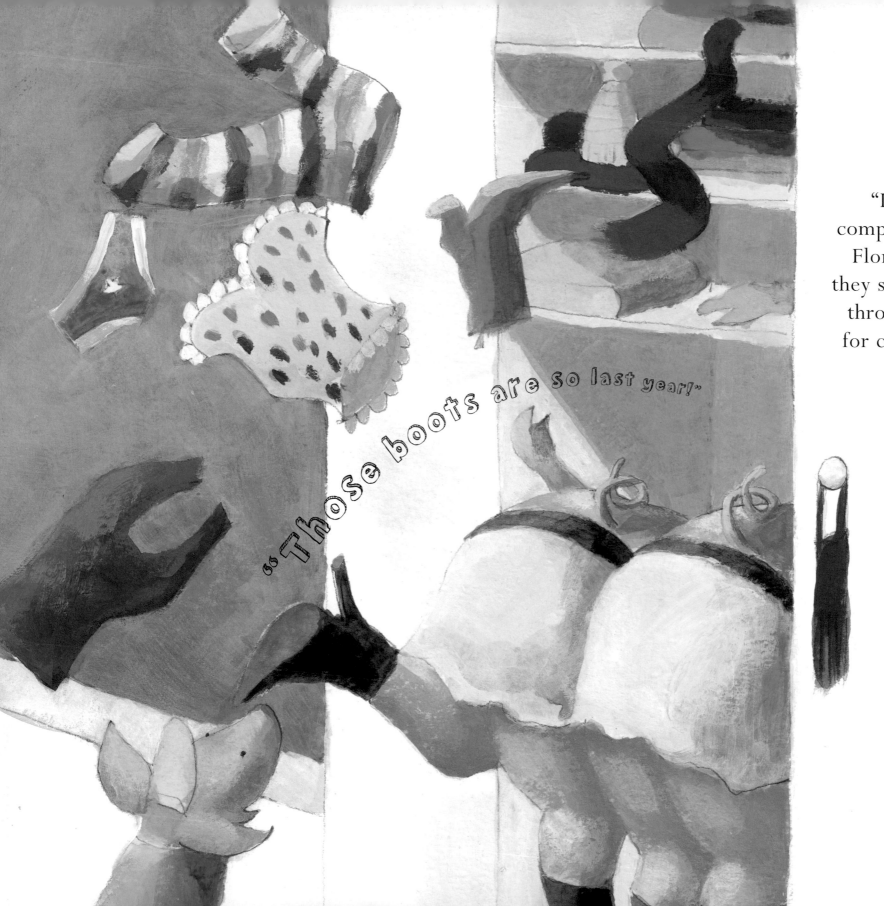

"Let's enter the competition!" squealed Florence's sisters as they started rummaging through their closets for costumes to wear.

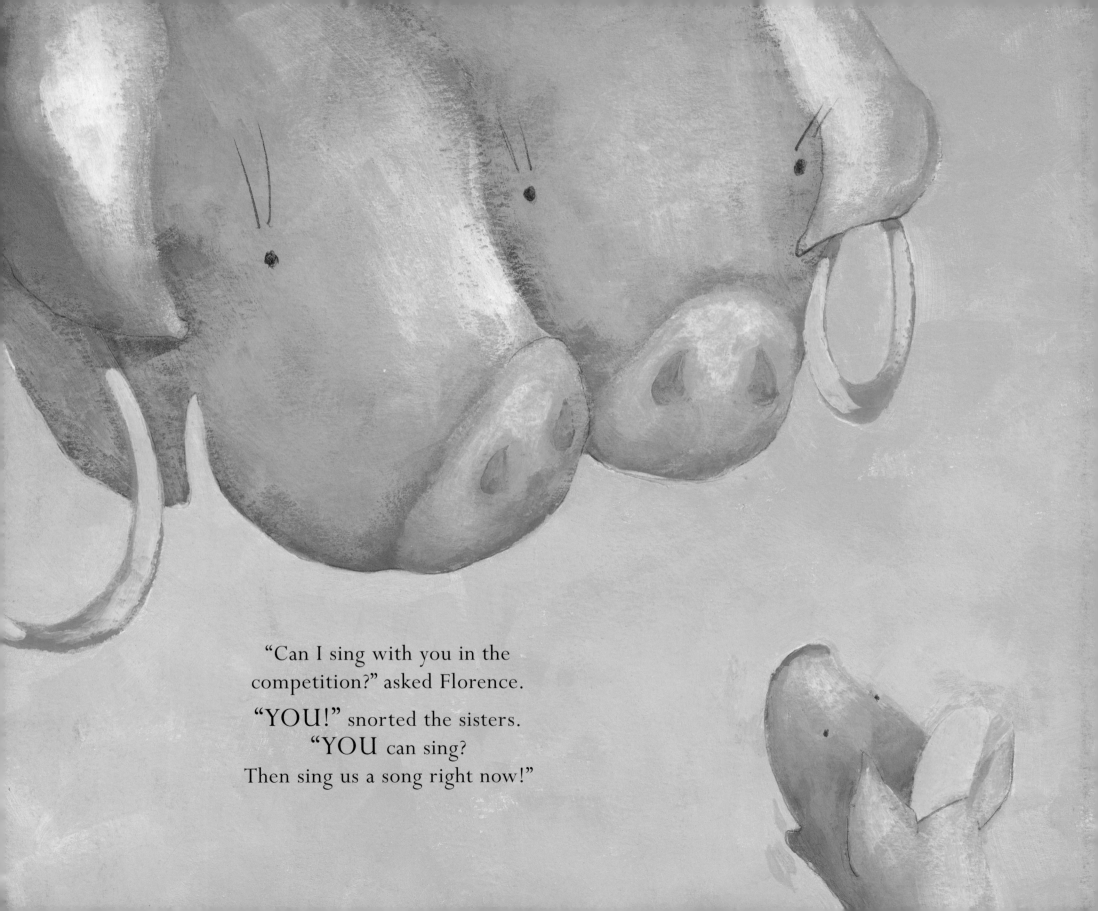

"Can I sing with you in the
competition?" asked Florence.

"YOU!" snorted the sisters.
"YOU can sing?
Then sing us a song right now!"

Florence took
a deep breath, raised
her head, and opened her little
snout. But as she looked up, she saw
her big sisters peering down at her. Suddenly,
she felt very small, and very, very shy, and very, very,
very nervous. And all she could manage was a teeny, tiny . . .

"Squeak!"

Her sisters
burst out laughing.
"You can't sing with
us in the competition.
You can't even *sing!*"

Florence was so sad.

Every day she asked her sisters if she could join
their singing practice, but every day they said,

"No."

All Florence could do was listen to
them rehearse. Soon she knew all the words
front to back and back to front and inside out.

Finally the day of the competition arrived.

The line outside the television studio
stretched for miles and miles.

At last the doors opened, and the first band played. The judges looked impressed and the crowd cheered. Florence waited excitedly for her sisters to appear.

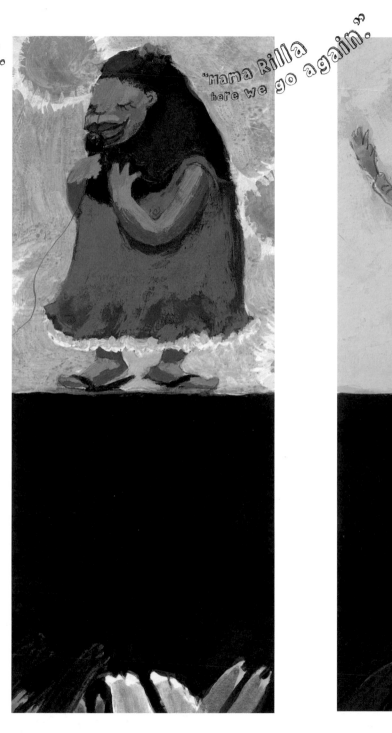

She waited and waited . . .

and waited . . .

and waited some more . . .

## until finally . . .

Florence's sisters burst
onto the stage singing
with all their might. But as
they sang they looked out into the . . .

large crowd
and they started to feel

very small.

Then they looked up and saw the . . .

TV cameras.
And they suddenly felt
very, very shy. And when
their eyes met with the . . .

beady eyes of the judges,
they felt so nervous they forgot
all the words to their song!
Everything went quiet . . .

until a small voice started
singing from the crowd.
"Find that voice!"
shouted the judges.

The spotlight went out over
the crowd, and guess who it found?

A small pink pig standing on
tiptoe, singing with all her might!

"Please come to the stage,
little pig!" called the judges.

Florence's sisters were
not laughing at her now.

And as she trotted up to the stage,
Florence did not feel small, or shy, or nervous.

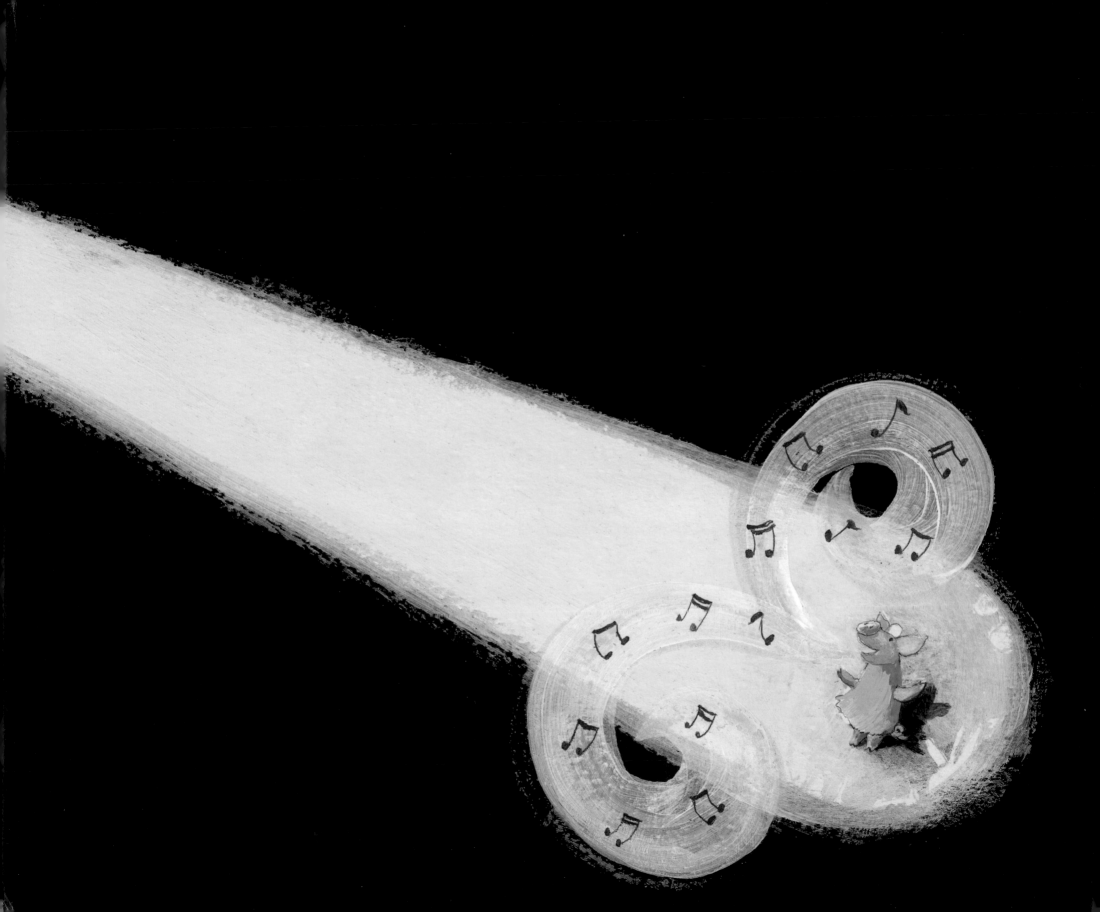

Florence was awarded First Prize.
And her dream of becoming a
piggy pop star was about to come true.

Florence topped the charts with songs about love, life, and vegetarianism. And as for her sisters, they never sang again, but they made sure all their friends knew just who their little sister was!

"That's our sister."

"we taught her everything she knows!"

MUSIC SHOP

MUSIC SHOP

No.1 SMALL FLORENCE

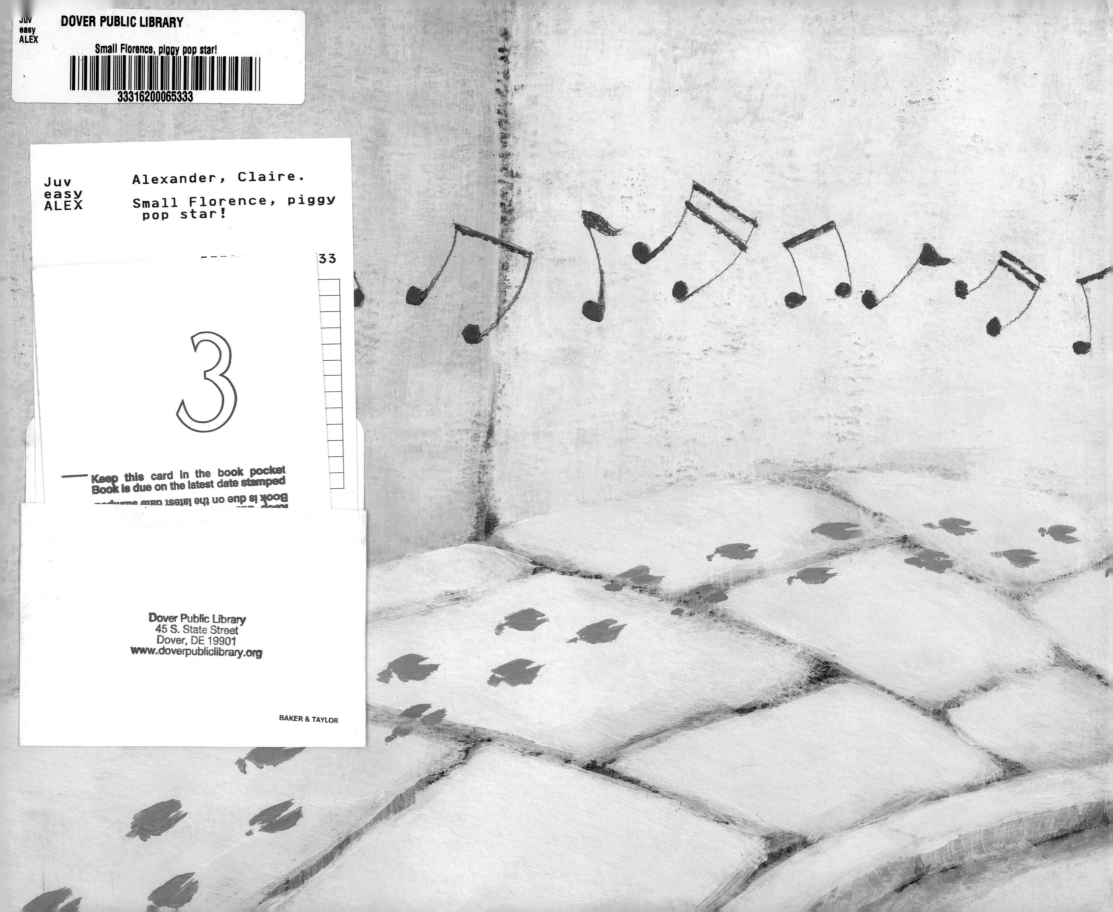